W9-CFG-086

DISCARD
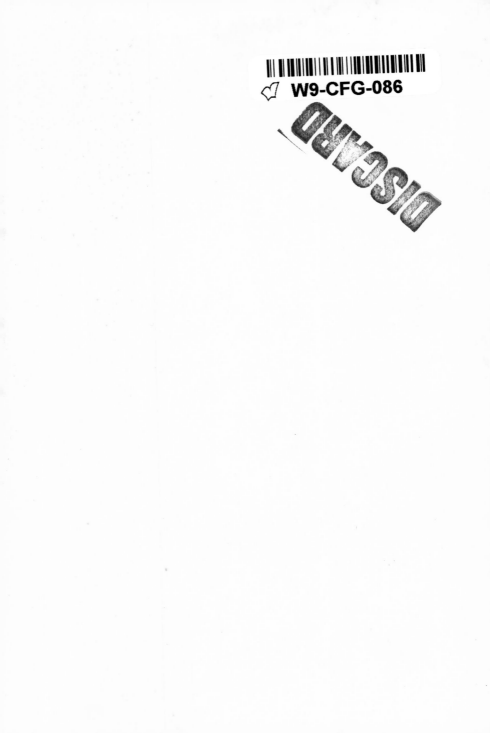

GIRL WONDER
AND THE
TERRIFIC TWINS

BY **Malorie Blackman**

ILLUSTRATED BY LIS TOFT

Dutton Children's Books

New York

WESTBOROUGH PUBLIC LIBRARY
WESTBOROUGH, MASSACHUSETTS

Text copyright © 1991 by Oneta Malorie Blackman
Illustrations copyright © 1991 by Lis Toft

All rights reserved. No part of this publication may be reproduced
or transmitted in any form or by any means, electronic or mechanical,
including photocopy, recording, or any information storage and retrieval
system now known or to be invented, without permission in writing from
the publisher, except by a reviewer who wishes to quote brief passages
in connection with a review written for inclusion in
a magazine, newspaper, or broadcast.

Library of Congress Cataloging-in-Publication Data

Blackman, Malorie.
Girl Wonder and the Terrific Twins/by Malorie Blackman;
illustrated by Lis Toft.—1st American ed.
p.   cm.
Summary: The plans that Maxine, the Girl Wonder,
and her younger brothers, the Terrific Twins, come up with
usually mean trouble for their mother.
ISBN 0-525-45065-3
[1. Brothers and sisters—Fiction.   2. Twins—Fiction.
3. Mother and child—Fiction.]   I. Toft, Lis, ill.   II. Title.
PZ7.B532337Gi   1993   [Fic]—dc20   92-27667   CIP   AC

First published in the United States 1993 by Dutton Children's Books,
a division of Penguin Books USA Inc.
375 Hudson Street, New York, New York 10014

Originally published in Great Britain 1991 by Victor Gollancz Ltd

Designed by Amy Berniker
Printed in U.S.A.
First American Edition
1 3 5 7 9 10 8 6 4 2

For Neil, with love and affection   M.B.

For Tim   L.T.

Contents

The Mission to
Rescue the Soccer Ball

"Mom, can we play catch in the yard?" I asked.

"Please, please," said my brother Anthony.

"Please, please," said my other brother, Edward.

Mom's head appeared from beneath the hood of her car. She wiped her oily hands on her coveralls.

"All right," Mom said. "But watch the fence by the tree, it's loose. And for goodness' sake, keep the ball away from Miss Ree's flowers."

Miss Ree is our grumpy old next-door neighbor. She has flowers growing all around her smooth-as-paper lawn. She complains if we even breathe near her flowers. We call her Misery. Miss Ree. Mis-e-ry. Get it?

1

The twins and I ran through the house, grabbed the ball, and ran out into the back-yard.

It was hot, hot, hot. We played keep away and catch for a while.

"I'm hot," complained Anthony.

"I'm bored," complained Edward.

"Let's play soccer," I suggested. "We'll each be a team. You only score a goal if you hit the trunk of the apple tree."

"Yeah! Soccer!" said Anthony.

"Yippee! Soccer!" said Edward.

We all like soccer.

I scored the first two goals, then Edward tripped me and Anthony got the ball.

"Cheats!" I shouted, chasing them.

Anthony kicked the ball as hard as he could.

"Ha! You missed," I shouted.

Anthony hadn't missed the tree trunk by inches. He'd missed it by miles. The ball sailed over the fence into Miss Ree's yard and landed with a *plop!* right in her flower bed.

Anthony, Edward, and I ran to the fence and looked over.

Oh, dear!

If we asked for our ball back, Miss Ree would complain to Mom and then we'd get told off.

So I said, "This is a job for Girl Wonder and . . ."

"The Terrific Twins! Hooray!" the twins shouted.

We all spun around until we felt giddy.

"Okay, Terrific Twins, I've got a plan," I

said. "We'll climb over the fence and I'll get the ball while you two watch for Misery. Make sure you warn me if she's coming."

"Okay, Girl Wonder," said Anthony.

So we all started to climb over the fence.

Crrrreak!

Crrrrunch!

The whole fence fell, right onto Miss Ree's flower bed. And with us on top of it! While we were sprawled out and wondering what had happened, Miss Ree's kitchen door burst open. Then our kitchen door flew open.

"My roses! My lupines! My begonias!" Miss Ree wailed.

"My goodness!" Mom said, running out of the kitchen.

"Just look what they've done to my flowers," Miss Ree said to Mom. Mom put her hands on her hips. Her face was like dark gray clouds just before thunder and lightning.

"Maxine, Anthony, Edward, what have you been doing now?" Mom said.

"We just wanted to get our ball, Mom," I said as we all stood up.

"I'm sorry about your flowers, Miss Ree," Mom said. "Don't worry. I'll fix the fence and we'll replace all the flowers."

Then Mom marched us into the house.

She told us off in the kitchen. She told us off in the car as we drove to the garden center. She told us off as we picked out new flowers. She told us off as we drove back home. She told us off as she fixed the fence. She told us off as we all pulled the scrunched, crushed flowers out of the ground and planted the new ones.

While Mom was resting her mouth for a second, I whispered to Anthony, "There's our ball. Run and get it and throw it back into our yard."

Before Mom could say anything, Anthony did just that.

Once we had planted Miss Ree's new flowers, Mom led us into the house again.

"Can we take our ball and go to the park?" I asked.

"No, you cannot. You three can stay in for the rest of the day and stay out of trouble," Mom said.

So after we'd washed our hands and faces and changed our clothes, the twins and I sat on the carpet in the living room playing go fish.

"Your plan was stupid," Anthony grumbled.

"Yeah! Silly-stupid," said Edward.

"But it worked, didn't it?" I said. "We did get our ball back!"

2
Keeping Cool at the Swimming Pool

It was bright, burning hot.

So hot the branches on our apple tree drooped.

So hot Miss Ree's flowers hung their heads.

So hot I was sure I was going to melt at any second. "What should we do today?" I muttered.

"It's too hot to do anything," Anthony murmured.

"Yeah! Too hot!" Edward mumbled.

Mom fanned herself with the newspaper. "We all need to do something to cool off. I know, let's go swimming."

"Swimming! Yeah!" I said.

"Swimming! Hooray!" Anthony shouted.

"Swimming! Yippee!" Edward clapped his hands. So we got our swimsuits and some towels and Mom drove us to the swimming pool. When we'd all changed into our swimsuits, Mom led us down to the pool.

"I want all three of you to stay near me," Mom said. "And don't go anywhere near the deep end."

The pool was jam-packed with kids. And all around the edge of the pool were moms and dads.

"Oh, dear! I should have realized it would be this crowded. Everyone had the same idea." Mom sighed.

We got into the pool at the shallow end. We couldn't even walk from one side of the pool to the other without bumping into someone, let alone swim. But at least we were wet and cool.

"It's so hot," said a woman standing by the pool.

"I wish I were in there. I'm so uncomfortable," said the man next to her.

I looked up at them. The woman wiped the sweat off her forehead while the man used his hand to fan himself. Everyone around the pool seemed really uncomfortable. They were all looking longingly at the water.

"Look at those people," I whispered to Anthony and Edward. "We should do something to cool them off."

"What?" Anthony asked.

"Yeah! What?" Edward repeated.

So I said, "I think this is a job for Girl Wonder and . . ."

"The Terrific Twins!" Anthony and Edward splashed up and down in the water. Then we spun around as fast as we could in the water—which wasn't fast at all, so we soon gave up.

"Okay, Terrific Twins, I have a plan," I said. "We're going to help cool off all those people around the pool."

"Why?" Anthony asked.

"Yeah! Why?" Edward repeated.

"Because we're superheroes. We should help people," I said.

"How?" Anthony asked.

"Yeah! How?" Edward repeated.

"How about if we jog past all those hot, sticky, sweaty people and splash them with drops of cold water? That would cool them off," I suggested.

"Good idea," said Anthony.

"Yeah! Good idea!" said Edward.

"Where are you going?" Mom asked as we got out of the pool.

"Just for a walk, Mom," I said.

"Well, be careful and stay away from the deep end," Mom replied.

We walked to the opposite corner of the pool.

"Ready, Terrific Twins?" I asked.

"Ready!"

The three of us formed a line and jogged along shaking our hands and heads as we went, splashing the grown-ups with water. I must admit, they didn't look very pleased.

Then Anthony bumped into a thin woman. Her arms spun around as she tried to keep her balance. She grabbed the man wearing glasses next to her, who grabbed the bald man next to him. The thin woman yelled as she plunged into the pool, followed by the man with glasses, then the bald man. As the bald man was falling he grabbed the arm of the woman next to him. Everyone was grab-

12

bing everyone else to stop themselves from falling into the pool, but it didn't help. The whole line of men and women tumbled into the water.

Splash!

"Oh, dear!" I muttered.

Mom came running up to us.

"Maxine, Anthony, Edward, what have you three rascals been doing now?" Mom asked. "You should have more sense than to run around a swimming pool. It's dangerous. You might have slipped."

I looked in the pool at all those men and women, coughing and sputtering and wringing out their shirts and jackets and dresses. They were all glaring at us. It looked like we were the only ones who hadn't slipped.

"What were you three doing?" Mom asked, her hands on her hips. But we didn't get the chance to explain. We got kicked out of the swimming pool by the lifeguard. Mom was so embarrassed.

All the way home all she kept saying was, "I'll never live this down. I'll never live this down."

"Your plan was feeble," Anthony mumbled.

"Yeah! Foolish-feeble," Edward grumbled.

"But it worked, didn't it?" I said. "We did cool off all those people."

3

Rescuing
the Rescuers

"I want a dog," I said.

"I want a cat," said Anthony.

"I want a rabbit," said Edward.

Mom put her hands on her hips. "I'm not getting three different pets. In fact, I'm not sure I should even get one."

"But . . . ," I said.

"But . . . ," said Anthony.

"But . . . ," Edward repeated.

"No buts!" Mom argued. "I don't think you three realize how much work is involved in owning a pet."

"We do!" I said.

"We do!" said Anthony.

"We do!" Edward repeated.

Then Mom got a funny look in her eyes. The same look she gets when she has one of her ideas and she thinks it's a good one.

15

I wonder why her ideas always seem to get me and the twins into trouble.

"Stay there, you three. I'll be right back," Mom said, and off she dashed.

My brothers and I looked at each other and shrugged. We started to get bored just standing and waiting. Then Mom came back with a large box in her hands.

"What's in the box?" we asked.

Mom put the box down on the carpet. We peered into it.

"A cat!" I said, surprised.

"It's Mr. McBain's cat. Her name is Syrup, because she's the same color as maple syrup."

Mr. McBain is our other next-door neighbor. He's a tall elderly man with hair that only grows on the sides of his head. The top of his head is shiny and smooth, like an egg.

"How come she's here?" Anthony asked.

"Yeah! How come?" asked Edward.

"If you three can look after Syrup this weekend without getting into trouble, then we'll talk seriously about which pet to get—but only then," Mom said.

"What do we do first?" I asked.

Anthony, Edward, and I knelt down around the box.

"First, take Syrup out of the box. Then put her litter box in the basement, near the washing machine. Then you can feed her. Mr. McBain also gave me two cans of cat food. They're in my pockets. After that you can play with her," Mom said.

So I took Syrup out of the box and held her against my chest and stroked her. She was warm, and her fur was soft. Her breath tickled my face. I liked her.

Maybe we should have a cat and not a dog, I thought.

Anthony took out Syrup's litter box and put it in the basement. Edward got the two cans of cat food out of Mom's pockets.

"Later on we'll go to the store at the end of the road and get some more cat food," said Mom.

She opened one of the cans and put the food in Syrup's bowl. We all crouched around Syrup as she ate.

"I want a cat, Mom," I said.

"So do I," Anthony said.

"Yeah! Me too!" said Edward.

"We'll see" was all Mom said.

After Syrup had eaten her lunch, we took her outside while Mom went to watch TV. I was still holding Syrup.

"Syrup, this is our yard," I said.

"Meow!" Syrup replied, looking around.

Then, before any of us had a chance to blink, Syrup struggled out of my arms, scurried across our yard, and scooted up our apple tree.

"What do we do now?" Anthony asked.

"Yeah! What?" asked Edward.

"We can't call Mom," I said. "She'll say we can't look after a pet for one minute without getting into trouble."

"So what are we going to do?" asked Anthony.

"Yeah! What?" Edward repeated.

So I said, "This is a job for Girl Wonder and . . ."

"The Terrific Twins!" Anthony and Edward said, grinning.

Then we all spun around until we were dizzy.

"All right, Terrific Twins, I have a plan," I said. "We'll climb up the tree and get Syrup down."

And that's what we did. Slowly and carefully, we climbed up the tree. (I helped the twins get onto the first branch, since they couldn't quite reach it.) Up and up we went. Up and up. Above I could see Syrup staring down at us.

Just as we got close to her, guess what she did?

She yawned. She stretched her back. Then she scooted down the tree.

"Hey! Why didn't she do that before we came up here?" I said.

We all looked down. The ground looked far, far away.

"What are you kids up to?" Mr. McBain called out from his yard.

"What do you children think you're doing?" shouted Miss Ree from her garden. "Get down right now, before you hurt yourselves."

I looked at Anthony and Edward, and they looked at me. Then we all burst into tears.

"We can't get down," I sobbed. "The ground is far, far away."

Then Mom came running out into the yard.

"Maxine, Anthony, Edward, what have you been doing now?" she said, her hands on her hips.

"We were trying to rescue the cat," I sniffed.

"Maxine, cats climb up trees all the time," Mr. McBain said. "Unlike you, they have no trouble climbing down, either. You should have left Syrup up there."

"Mom, I want to come down," wailed Anthony.

"Yeah! Me too!" Edward joined in.

"I'm going to have to call the fire department," Mom said.

Within minutes we heard the sound of the fire-engine siren—*wheer wheer wheer wheer!* Mom ran into the house to let them in. Seconds later she came out into the yard followed by four fire fighters. They all stood below our apple tree. We peered down at them. We'd never seen fire fighters up close before. They placed two ladders against the trunk of the tree.

"It's all right. We'll get you down," said one of the fire fighters.

"Don't worry," said another. "You'll soon be on the ground."

They carried Anthony and Edward down first. I looked around. I could see across all the neighbors' yards. Everyone was watching us.

"All right, Maxine, take my hands," said a fire fighter, lifting me onto her back. "I'm going to give you a piggyback ride."

"A piggyback ride! In a tree?" I laughed nervously.

"You're lucky. In a fire, I'd only have time to sling you over one shoulder," she said. "Here we are, down on the ground."

I looked around, surprised. I hadn't even noticed coming down.

"Say thank you to the fire fighters," Mom said.

"Thank you very much," we said.

"Now, you three go into the house. I've got a few things to say to you," Mom said sternly. "And Syrup is going right back to Mr. McBain."

We went into the kitchen and looked out the window. Mom was talking to the fire fighters.

"She's going to yell at us forever," Anthony said to me, annoyed.

"Yeah! Forever!" Edward agreed.

"Your plan was stinky," Anthony grumbled.

"Yeah! Serious-stinky," Edward mumbled.

"But it worked, didn't it?" I said. "We did get Syrup out of the tree."

Captain,
the Teddy-Bear Dog

The next day we decided to try again. *We wanted a pet!*

"Mom . . . ," Anthony said slowly. "We're sorry about what happened yesterday."

"Yeah, we're sorry," Edward said.

"Very sorry," I added.

"Hhmm!" was all Mom said.

"Can we have another chance, please?" Anthony asked. "I'd do anything to get a cat."

"A rabbit," said Edward.

"A—," I started to say.

"A nothing," Mom interrupted, her hands on her hips. "I have no intention of getting a pet for you three. Not after I had to call out the fire department yesterday. You had that cat for just five minutes, and you still managed to get into trouble."

"Oh, please," we all begged.

"*No!* And that's final." Mom turned back to her cooking.

My brothers and I wandered out into the yard. We sat on the ground, and I started to pull up blades of grass.

"It's all your fault, Maxine," Anthony said, frowning at me. "It was your idea to go up the tree after Syrup."

"Yeah, your fault," Edward agreed.

"No, it wasn't."

"Yes, it was."

"No, it wasn't."

"Yes, it was."

Then we had a big argument about whose fault it was, until Mom tapped on the kitchen window and made a stern face that said, *I hope you three aren't arguing* without the words even having to come out of her mouth.

"The thing is, what are we going to do now?" I said. "We've got to persuade Mom to buy us a pet."

"That's a hard one," said Anthony.

"Yeah! Hard!" agreed Edward.

"I think this is definitely a job for Girl Wonder and . . ."

"The Terrific Twins," said Anthony and Edward glumly.

This was definitely a tough one! We sat and thought and thought.

"Terrific Twins, I've got it!" I said at last, clapping my hands together. "We'll prove to Mom that we can look after a pet."

"She'll never allow us to have Syrup back," Anthony said. "So how are we going to look after a pet without actually having a pet to practice on?"

"Yeah! How?" asked Edward.

"We'll use Captain, my teddy bear, and pretend he's a dog."

"A cat," said Anthony.

"A rabbit," said Edward.

"Do you two want to hear my plan or not?" I asked, folding my arms across my chest.

"Well, hurry up, then," Anthony said.

"Yeah, hurry up," Edward added.

Brothers!

"As I was saying, we'll have to pretend Captain is our pet and show Mom that we can take care of him. And Captain will be a dog, because he's my teddy bear and it was my idea."

So we agreed and went indoors to start our plan. I ran upstairs and brought Captain down. I put him in front of the TV.

"You three are very quiet," Mom said as she walked into the room. Then she saw Captain. "Maxine, why have you brought your teddy bear downstairs?"

"Captain is our pet dog," Anthony said.

A slow smile spread over Mom's face. "So you'll need to take him for a walk now," she said.

"That's right," I replied, annoyed because Mom was biting her bottom lip. She always does that when she's trying not to laugh.

Mom went out into the kitchen and came back with a piece of string with a loop at one end. "There you are, a leash for your dog," she said, biting her lip again.

I put the leash around Captain's neck.

"Come on, you two, we've got to take Captain for a walk," I said.

"I'm not walking down the street dragging a teddy bear." Anthony frowned.

"Me neither," said Edward.

"I thought it was a dog." Mom laughed.

"It's a dog in the house," Anthony said. "Outside the house it's a teddy bear."

Anthony and Edward refused to take Captain for a walk with me. So that was the end of that idea. When Mom had left the room I said, "All right. We'll have to come up with another plan to persuade Mom to buy us a pet."

"Like what?" Anthony asked.

"Such as?" asked Edward.

5

Get a Pet: Plan Two

"If we want a pet, we're going to have to come up with a super-duper-fantastic plan," I replied. "So this is a job that only Girl Wonder and . . ."

"The Terrific Twins can do," Edward finished, and we all spun around until the room spun with us.

We sat very still and thought very hard.

"How about . . . ," I began slowly. "How about if we're very good and help Mom around the house, and then she'll forget about yesterday?"

"Hhmm!" said Anthony.

"Hhhmmm!" Edward repeated.

"It's worth a try, unless either of you has a better idea."

They didn't. We walked into the kitchen.

"Do you want some help, Mom?" we asked.

"Some help doing what?" Mom asked suspiciously.

"Some help washing the dishes," I answered.

Mom looked really suspicious now. "There are only three saucepans and a couple of plates, but all right. Edward and Anthony, you can wash, and Maxine, you can dry."

"All right, Mom," we said.

Mom put her hands on her hips. "What are you three up to now?"

"Nothing. We're just helping you—that's all."

"Hhmm!" Mom replied. "All right, but no messing around."

Anthony put on Mom's rubber gloves as Mom left the kitchen, shaking her head.

"Don't drop any plates," I hissed at the twins.

Anthony started to fill the sink with warm water. Then he squeezed some dish-washing liquid under the faucets—and he squeezed and he *squeezed*. The bump of bubbles in the sink grew into a hill of bubbles. We stared at the mountain of bubbles, which was still growing.

"How much soap did you squeeze into the sink?" I asked Anthony.

"All of it." Anthony frowned. "Wasn't I supposed to?"

"I don't think so," I replied. "Quick, do something."

Edward swept his hand through the bubbles. They flew everywhere—up toward the ceiling and down toward the floor.

"Maxine, do something," Anthony said quickly.

Then the water in the sink began to splash over onto the kitchen floor.

"Turn off the faucets. Quick!" I said.

Anthony turned off the faucets, but it was too late. The water squelched and slurped under our feet.

"That's the end of my cat." Anthony sighed.

"That's the end of my rabbit." Edward shrugged.

"Get some kitchen towels," I said quickly. "Don't let Mom see this—"

"Don't let Mom see what?"

We all spun around. There was Mom in the kitchen doorway, her hands on her hips.

"Maxine! Anthony! Edward!" Mom roared. "What have you done to the kitchen?" She pointed to the super-enormous universe of bubbles behind us and to the puddle under our feet.

"We . . . er . . ."

"Never mind. Anthony, pull out the plug in the bottom of the sink," Mom ordered. Then she stood over us as we mopped the floor and wiped the sink and the counters, which took ages. And of all the yelling Mom has ever done, the shouting she did as we cleaned up the kitchen was the best! (By that I mean the most annoyed!) We tried to tell Mom that we'd only been trying to help, but she wouldn't listen.

"Trying to help!" she fumed. "Trying to help! A hurricane would have been more helpful."

"Does that mean you won't buy us a pet?" Anthony asked. I could have kicked him.

"So that's what this is all about," Mom retorted. "All right, that does it. Tomorrow I'm going to get you a pet, and that'll be the end of it."

"Get a cat. Please, please," pleaded Anthony.

"No, don't. Get a rabbit. Please, Mom," begged Edward.

"A dog would be the most interesting, Mom," I began.

Mom raised her hand. "That's enough from all three of you. I have already made up my mind which pet we're going to have."

We tried to ask Mom which pet she was going to get, but all she said was, "Ask me no questions and I'll tell you no lies."

And Mom didn't mention our pet for the rest of the day.

The next morning we peered out of the window, waiting for Mom to return from the pet store. At last she came walking up the path with a small brown bag in her hand.

"That's much too little for a kitten." Anthony frowned.

"That bag is too tiny for a rabbit," said Edward.

"That bag is too puny for a puppy," I said.

We ran out to meet Mom.

"What is it? What is it?" we asked eagerly.

Mom pulled off the brown bag. In her hand she held a small plastic bag filled with water, and in the water was a tiny goldfish.

"This is your pet," Mom said.

A goldfish!

"The tank is in the car next to the fish food on the passenger seat. Maxine, you get the tank and carry it *carefully*. Boys, you can get the fish food."

"A goldfish!" Anthony said when we got to the car. "That's not much of a pet. It can't catch mice like a cat."

"Or munch lettuce and carrots like a rabbit," said Edward.

"Or fetch a stick like a dog." I sighed.

"So much for your silly-stupid-stinky-smelly plan, Maxine." Anthony pouted.

"Hey!" I replied. "We got a pet, didn't we? And a goldfish is better than nothing."

As Tall as Tall

I was in a bad mood when I got home from school.

"What's the matter with you?" Anthony asked.

"Yeah, what's the matter?" asked Edward.

I stared at myself in the hall mirror. I turned to the left and I turned to the right.

"Do you think I'm short?" I asked my brothers.

"You're taller than us," said Anthony.

"A lot taller," agreed Edward.

"But I'm not as tall as Sharon, this girl in my class. She's taller than everyone—except the teacher."

"So?" said Anthony.

"She called me shorty." I frowned. "I need to grow taller—a lot taller. I want to be taller than Sharon. I want to be as tall as tall."

"How are you going to do that?" Anthony asked.

"Yeah, how?" asked Edward.

"I'll have to think about that one," I replied.

"Maybe this is a job for Girl Wonder and . . ."

"The Terrific Twins!" my brothers shouted, whirling around like spinning tops.

"We need a plan—something that will make me grow," I said. "Come on, Terrific Twins, I need your help. Think!"

We sat down on the carpet with our legs crossed. We each sat very still and thought and thought. I thought so hard that my head began to ache.

"How tall do you want to grow?" asked Anthony. "Do you want to grow as tall as a mountain or only as tall as a tree?"

I thought for a moment. "As tall as a tree," I decided. That would be tall enough.

We each thought some more.

"Well, if you plant a little seed, it grows into a big tree," Edward said. "So maybe if you swallowed a little seed, it would grow into a big tree inside you, and it would push you up and up and then you'd be as tall as a tree. You'd be as tall as tall."

"That's a good idea!" I said, grinning. "I'll swallow orange seeds. Orange trees are tall, and I can get the seeds because we always have plenty of oranges in the house. Are you two going to join me?"

"Nah! We'll watch you first to see if it works," Anthony said.

"Yeah, we'll watch you first," Edward agreed.

Just then Mom came in from the garage.

"All right, what would you three like for dinner?" Mom asked.

"French fries," said Anthony.

"Hot dogs and french fries," said Edward, clapping his hands.

"Oranges!" I shouted.

Mom just laughed. I think she thought I was joking.

In the end Mom made fish and french fries. I didn't have any, even though it smelled yummy-delicious. I had to leave room for my oranges. While the twins and Mom munched the yummy-delicious fish and french fries, I ate my oranges, swallowing the seeds whole.

"Why are you eating so many oranges?" Mom asked me.

"I like oranges," I replied, trying to force down the last one.

Mom looked at me suspiciously. All she said was, "Hhmm!"

The next day I had two oranges for breakfast, three oranges for lunch, and four oranges for dinner. Then I measured myself on our growth chart in the bathroom. I hadn't grown one inch! And what's more, I was sick—sick of oranges.

When I woke up the next morning, I had the worst tummy ache in the world.

"Ooh!" I groaned. "Ooooh!"

Mom called the doctor.

"Now then, Maxine," Dr. Turner said after taking my temperature, "your mom told me that you're eating a lot of oranges. She said you're eating oranges and nothing else. Is that right?"

I nodded. Oooooooh! My stomach really hurt.

"Why have you suddenly become so fond of oranges?" Dr. Turner asked.

Mom was standing by Dr. Turner, waiting for me to answer. She had her hands on her hips.

"I love oranges." I didn't exactly lie, but I didn't exactly tell the truth, either.

"Is that the whole reason?" Mom asked softly.

I thought hard. My stomachache was getting worse, and I was as miserable as miserable, but I didn't want to tell Mom why I was eating so many oranges. She might stop me, or worse still she might be annoyed with me.

"Yeah, that's the whole reason," I replied.

"Dr. Turner, can I speak to you for a moment?" Mom said.

The doctor and my mom went out into the hallway.

"I . . . oranges . . . cure . . . oranges . . . oranges . . . oranges . . ." That was all I heard, even though I pushed my ears as far forward as possible.

Mom and Dr. Turner came back into the room.

"Maxine, Dr. Turner agrees with me that what you need is a diet of oranges and nothing else," Mom began. "I was going to make you a grilled cheese sandwich, followed by ice cream and chocolate sauce and a tall glass of ice-cold ginger ale, but . . ."

"It's all right," I said quickly. "I don't mind having that."

"Nonsense." Mom smiled. "You said you love oranges. That's all you've eaten for the last two days."

"But just to make sure that Maxine gets all her essential vitamins and minerals, I would

prescribe two tablespoons of cod-liver oil three times a day and a vitamin twice a day," said Dr. Turner, scribbling on a pad. "That way Maxine can eat as many oranges as she likes and nothing else."

"No! I don't want any more oranges," I pleaded. "Maybe . . . maybe I don't like them so much after all."

"Then why were you eating so many of them?" Mom asked.

Her eyes were sparkling like sunshine on

water. When she looks at me like that, it's as if she can read my mind. I decided that perhaps I should just tell the truth. The truth takes a lot less effort.

"Well . . . Sharon at school called me a shorty," I muttered. "So I was swallowing orange seeds so that they would grow into a tree inside me and push me up. Then I'd be taller than Sharon, and she couldn't call me a shorty anymore."

"Oh, I see." Dr. Turner laughed.

"Oh, I see." Mom smiled.

"Maxine, it's the oranges that are causing your stomachache," Dr. Turner said. "And it doesn't matter how many you eat, you'll never get a tree to grow inside of you. If you want to grow, you have to eat lots of different kinds of foods, like carrots and green vegetables and eggs and milk."

"Yuck!" I said. "What about chocolate? Will that make me grow?"

"Only sideways, not upward," said Dr. Turner with a smile.

"Maxine, you're not short, and it wouldn't matter if you were," Mom said. "It's what you are inside that counts, not what you are outside. Do you understand?"

"Yes, Mom," I said, holding my aching stomach.

"Okay, Maxine, I'll prescribe some medicine for you that should take away your stomachache. No more oranges, or you'll turn into one," said Dr. Turner, making a face.

I smiled up at her. She's funny.

Mom went downstairs, followed by the doctor. After a few minutes Mom came back up the stairs alone, with her hands behind her back.

"I've brought you a drink," she said. Mom smiled, her eyes shining.

"What is it?" I asked suspiciously.

Mom brought out the glass from behind her back. "Orange juice!" She laughed.

I buried my head under my pillow. "Take it away!" I said. "I never want to see anything that's orange ever again."

7

Saving Energy

When I got home from school, I ran into the kitchen, where Mom was mashing potatoes for our dinner and the twins were setting the table.

"What did you do at school today?" Mom asked me.

"We learned about energy and how we should all save it," I replied, dropping my schoolbag on the kitchen floor. "We should always switch off lights when we're not in the room, and we should switch off all electric appli . . . appli . . . appliances when we're not using them."

"That's right," Mom said. "But I've been telling you and your brothers to save energy for years, and you haven't listened to one word yet."

"Oh, we will now," I said.

"Why?" Anthony asked.

"Yeah, why?" Edward repeated.

"Because the more energy we save, the less we waste, and the longer it will last us."

"How do we waste it?" Anthony asked.

"Well . . . ," I began.

"Maxine means that you shouldn't leave the refrigerator door open while you decide what you want to eat. A lot of cold air escapes, and it takes more energy for the fridge to cool off again," Mom said.

"Hhmm!" Edward said.

"Maxine, could you spoon the mashed potatoes onto the plates? I'll be right back."

When Mom left the room, I said to the twins, "I think we should make sure that we save energy."

"How?" Edward asked, for once getting in before Anthony.

"Hhmm!" I said. "We're going to need a good plan. I think maybe this is a job for Girl Wonder and . . ."

"The Terrific Twins! Yippee!" shouted the twins. And we spun around until we all fell down.

"How about . . . how about if we make sure that everything is switched off before we go to bed tonight?" Anthony suggested.

"We could go into each room and make sure that all the lights and things are switched off," Edward continued.

"That sounds like a good idea." I grinned. "All right then, I'll do the upstairs, and you two can do the downstairs."

"How come we get the downstairs?" Anthony protested.

"Yeah, how come?" repeated Edward.

"Because the downstairs is bigger, and there are two of you," I explained.

"Hhmm!" they both said, but they didn't argue, so I got away with it.

After our dinner, we sat down to watch TV.

"Mom, shouldn't we switch off the TV to save energy?" Edward asked.

Mom laughed. "But we're watching it. We can't save energy by switching it off and watch it at the same time."

"But it would save energy if we did switch it off, wouldn't it?" Edward persisted.

"Yes, it would," Mom agreed. "But I'm not going to. This is a good show."

Edward leaned over and whispered to Anthony and me, "Let's not watch it. Let's do something else. Then we'll be saving energy."

"I don't think it works that way." I frowned. "The TV uses the same amount of energy whether Mom watches it alone or all four of us watch it."

So we watched TV until it was time for us to go to bed.

"I think I'll make this an early night as well." Mom yawned, switching off the TV.

We brushed our teeth and put on our pajamas. Then, when Mom was in the bathroom, I grabbed my brothers.

"Come on, Terrific Twins. Now's our chance to save energy. You two do the downstairs, and I'll do the bedrooms," I said.

Five minutes later we met back upstairs.

"We've saved energy everywhere," the twins said proudly.

"So have I," I said. "Good night, An-

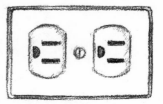

thony, good night, Edward. See you in the morning."

Mom read to the twins first, then she came into my bedroom and read me a fairy tale. I love fairy tales.

"Good night, Maxine," Mom said, and she switched off the bedroom light and closed the door behind her. Then I fell asleep, dreaming of the ways I could save energy.

"Maxine, Anthony, Edward—get down here! This minute!"

I rubbed my eyes. It was morning, but I was still sleepy.

"Maxine! Edward! Anthony! Now!"

I didn't like the sound of Mom's voice. It sounded angrier than angry. I hopped out of bed and walked down the stairs behind the twins.

"What's the matter?" I whispered to them.

"I don't know," Anthony whispered back.

"Me neither," Edward mouthed.

We walked into the kitchen, where Mom stood with her hands folded across her chest, glaring at us.

I knew we were in *big trouble.*

"Which one of you numskulls unplugged the fridge last night?" Mom asked.

I looked at the twins. They looked at me. No one spoke.

"I'm waiting for an answer," Mom said. "I'll have you know that all the ice in the

freezer has melted because one of you three pulled out the plug for the fridge. The ice cream has melted all over the hamburger, and the fridge is one great big sticky mess. It's full of water. And look at this water all over the floor!"

Still no one said a word.

"And which one of you nitwits switched off the washing machine when it was in the middle of washing my sweaters?" Mom demanded. "Now all my sweaters have shrunk. They're ruined."

The twins and I looked at each other. We stayed silent.

"And which one of you knuckleheads pulled out the plug for the VCR? I wanted to tape a late-night movie and I missed it!"

Anthony started to sniff, then to sob. "I . . . I pulled out the plug for the fridge. I was only trying to save energy like Maxine said. And I was . . . I was the one who pulled out . . . pulled out the VCR plug."

Edward started to howl. "I pulled out the plug for the washing machine. I was only

trying to save energy like Maxine said we
should."

"I never told you to pull out every plug in
the house," I protested. "Mom, that's not
fair."

"That's enough." Mom's hands were on
her hips. "All three of you are going to clean
up this kitchen until it's spotless. And no
more allowance for the three of you until
you've paid for my ruined sweaters."

And Mom marched out of the kitchen.

We got out the mop and some sponges and
started wiping up the water on the floor.

"It's all your fault," Anthony said.

"Yeah, all your fault," Edward agreed. "You were the one who came home and said we should save energy."

"It was your idea to check and make sure we'd saved energy before we went to bed," I told the twins.

"But it was all your idea in the first place," Anthony said.

"I'm not talking to you two," I said in a huff.

"And we're not talking to you, either," Anthony replied. "Your idea was super-duper-gigantic-galactic-stinky. We didn't save our energy. My arms are killing me."

"Mine too," Edward agreed, giving me a dirty look.

Sometimes being a superhero is no fun!

8

Beware
the Park Bench

We were going to Aunt Joanne and Uncle Stan's house.

Their house is neat and clean and really boring! They don't have a single book on the floor. They don't have any comics on the chairs. Their kitchen never has dirty forks and spoons in the sink. It's not like our house at all.

We always have to dress up in our best clothes when we visit Uncle Stan and Aunt Joanne. Even Mom dresses up.

Since it was a sunny day, Mom decided that we could walk through the park. Our aunt and uncle live just on the other side. So off we went.

"Maxine, Anthony, Edward, make sure you keep your clothes spotless," Mom warned. "No messing around."

As if we would!

The park was full of people.

"Mom, can I go on the swings?" I asked. "Please, please?"

"No. You'll get your dress dirty," replied Mom.

"Mom, can I go on the merry-go-round?" Anthony asked.

"Yeah! The merry-go-round," Edward repeated.

"No. You'll wrinkle your clothes," Mom said.

I didn't see the point of going through the park if we couldn't run and jump and play in the playground.

"Oh, look at that," I said.

Near us, a girl and a boy were flying a kite. It danced in the sky. We all stopped to watch.

"Mom, do you know how to make a kite?" I asked.

"Yes. I'll show you when we get back home. It's really easy," Mom said.

"Hooray!" we all shouted.

That cheered us up.

We were just passing by a park bench when I noticed something very strange. There were two spiders trying to swing down from the bench, but they weren't getting very far. They scurried a little way along the bench and then tried to swing down, but they couldn't get all their legs off the bench. Then they scurried farther along and tried again, but the same thing happened.

"Mom, look at that." I pointed.

"How strange!" Mom said. "They can't get down."

And we all stopped to watch the spiders.

"Anthony, Edward, do you know what I think?" I whispered to them.

"No, what?" Anthony asked.

"Yeah! What?" Edward repeated.

So I said, "I think this is a job for Girl Wonder and . . ."

"The Terrific Twins!" my brothers whispered back.

And we spun around until the park was spinning with us.

"What on earth are you three doing?" Mom laughed.

"It's a secret," I told Mom.

"Well, come on. We can't stay here all day," Mom said.

"But Mom, can't we help the spiders?" Anthony asked.

"Yeah! Can't we do something? They want to get down," Edward said.

"Oh, all right," Mom replied.

She doesn't like spiders much. We all sat down on the bench and watched the spiders some more. Then I saw a piece of brown cardboard propped up against the side of the park bench.

"I've got a plan," I said to the twins as I leaned over to get it. "This piece of cardboard will help the spiders get to the ground."

I leaned one end of the cardboard against the bench and placed the other end against the ground so that the piece of cardboard was like a slide.

"Come on, Mr. and Mrs. Spider," I said. "We haven't got all day."

"No, we haven't," Mom agreed, glancing down at her watch.

61

The spiders hopped onto the cardboard immediately and scurried down to the ground.

"Come on," Mom said, and she started to stand up. Only she had trouble. She was sticking to the bench.

"What on earth . . . ," Mom said.

She put her hand down on the bench. Then she looked at the palm of her hand. It was bright green.

"This bench is wet!" Mom said, springing up off the bench. "Stand up, you three."

We stood up.

"Turn around," Mom ordered.

We turned around.

"Oh, no!" Mom cried. "Just look at your best clothes!"

We twisted our heads to look at our backs. I pulled the back of my skirt out to look at it. It was covered in green paint.

"Why didn't they leave a sign here to warn people that the bench had just been painted?" Mom asked furiously, her hands on her hips.

She was seriously, seriously annoyed!

Then she looked down at the cardboard slide I had used to help the spiders get to

the ground. She picked it up and turned it over. Then she showed it to us. There on the sign, in big green letters, it said:

BEWARE!! WET PAINT!!

"Maxine, why didn't you read this sign before we all sat down and ruined our clothes? That's why the spiders couldn't get down. Their feet kept sticking to the paint," Mom said. "Come on. We're going to have to go home and change."

"Look at what you've done to my terrific pants," Anthony said to me.

"Yeah! Look at my super-terrific pants," Edward said. "They're ruined."

"Your plan was useless," Anthony said.

"Yeah! Super-useless," said Edward.

"But it worked, didn't it?" I said. "After all, we did get the spiders off the bench."

9

We Hate Shopping!

Mom dragged us shopping with her.

We hate shopping.

I pushed the grocery cart while Mom read off her shopping list and Anthony and Edward got the cans and packages from the shelves.

"Anthony, could you get me some all-purpose flour, please?" Mom said, pointing to the right shelf. "It's in the blue package."

Anthony picked up the package around its middle.

The top of the package broke open and *whoosh!* Flour flew up, all over Anthony's face.

Anthony coughed and sputtered and sputtered and coughed. Edward and I cracked up laughing.

It was funny! Anthony looked like a ghost.

"I can't take you anywhere," Mom hissed at Anthony as she wiped the white flour off his face.

We moved down the aisle. This time Anthony was pushing the cart, and Edward and I were getting the cans and packages.

"Maxine, could you get me some free-range eggs and check them all to make sure they're not cracked?" Mom said.

I picked up the first carton of free-range eggs I saw. The trouble was, I picked up the carton from the top, and it wasn't shut properly. The egg carton swung open and *splat!* All the eggs dropped to the floor, right on the foot of the woman standing next to me.

"I'm sorry. It wasn't my fault, the carton was already open," I said quickly.

Anthony and Edward were holding their stomachs, they were laughing so hard.

"I'm so sorry," Mom said to the woman with the eggy shoes.

Mom glared down at me. She had her hands on her hips and her eyes were squeezed together and her lips were a thin line.

Boy, was she annoyed!

"It's all right, madam. I'll clean this up," said a man holding a bucket and a mop.

"I'm sorry about the mess," Mom said, grabbing my hand. "Maxine, I can't take you anywhere."

I hate shopping.

Mom made me help Anthony push the cart.

"Edward, could you get me two bottles of soda?" Mom asked.

Edward picked up two plastic bottles. Mom went to look for orange juice. Edward put one bottle in the cart, but the other one slipped and dropped to the floor.

Boing! Boing!

To our surprise, the bottle bounced.

"I didn't know soda bottles did that," I said.

Edward picked it up and dropped it again.

Boing! Boing!

"Edward, what do you think you're doing?" Mom said, snatching the bottle out of my brother's hand.

With a frown she turned the bottle cap.

Ssssploosh! The soda sprayed everywhere. Over Edward, over Anthony, over me—and all over the four people standing behind us.

The twins and I laughed until our stomachs hurt and our eyes were watering.

"I . . . I was . . . er . . . just checking the bottle top to make sure it was on tight," Mom stammered. "I'm so sorry. Come on, you three. I can't take any of you anywhere!"

Mom dragged us away to the cash registers.

"I've never been so embarrassed." Mom shook her finger at all of us. "Edward, you should never shake bottles or cans of soda,

because when you open them they explode all over the place."

Mom told us off the entire time we were in line waiting to pay for our food. We still thought it was funny until Mom said we couldn't have any candy, because we had misbehaved. Then Mom made all three of us push the cart out of the store.

"It's the only way to keep all of your hands out of trouble," Mom said.

We walked out into the parking lot toward our car.

Suddenly someone shouted, "Stop those men!"

We looked around and saw a policeman

and a policewoman chasing two men—and they were all running in our direction.

"Stop those men!" the policewoman shouted again.

The men were getting closer to us.

Just as they were about to run past us, the twins and I gave our cart a huge shove.

The two men ran right into it. The blond man went flying over our cart while the man with brown hair fell into it.

The policeman and policewoman came running up, and then more police arrived from all directions. They grabbed hold of the two men and led them away.

Then two of the police came over to us, bringing our cart.

"Good job!" the policewoman said to us. "What are your names?"

The twins and I looked at each other.

So I said, "I'm Girl Wonder, and . . ."

"We're the Terrific Twins!" said Anthony and Edward together.

Hooray!

WESTBOROUGH PUBLIC LIBRARY

A22401 255286

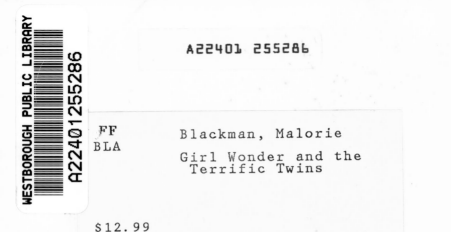

FF
BLA

Blackman, Malorie

Girl Wonder and the
Terrific Twins

$12.99

DATE			

WESTBOROUGH PUBLIC

LIBRARY

Westborough, Massachusetts